MASSACRE AT PARIS

By Christopher Marlowe

CONTENTS

Table of Contents with inital stage directions

DRAMATIS PERSONAE

THE MASSACRE AT PARIS.

Table of Contents with inital stage directions:
Dramatis Personae

Scene 13: Enter the Duchesse of Guise, and her Maide.

Scene 14: Enter the King of Navarre, Pleshe and Bartus, and their train, with drums and trumpets.

Scene 15: Enter [Henry] the King of France, Duke of Guise, Epernoune, and Duke Joyeux.

Scene 16: Alarums within. The Duke Joyeux slaine.

Scene 17: Enter a Souldier.

Scene 18: Enter the King of Navarre reading of a letter, and Bartus.

Scene 19: Enter the Captaine of the guarde, and three murtherers.

Scene 20: Enter two [Murtherers] dragging in the Cardenall [of Loraine].

Scene 21: Enter Duke Dumayn reading of a letter, with others.

Scene 22: Sound Drumme and Trumpets, and enter the King of France,
and Navarre, Epernoune, Bartus, Pleshe and Souldiers.

DRAMATIS PERSONAE
   CHARLES THE NINTH—King of France
   Duke of Anjou—his brother, afterwards KNIG HENRY THE THIRD
   King of Navarre
   PRINCE OF CONDE—his brother

   brothers
   DUKE OF GUISE

3

CARDINAL OF LORRAINE
DUKE DUMAINE

SON TO THE DUKE OF GUISE—a boy
THE LORD HIGH ADMIRAL
DUKE OF JOYEUX
EPERNOUN
PLESHE
BARTUS
TWO LORDS OF POLAND
GONZAGO
RETES
MOUNTSORRELL
COSSINS,—Captain of the King's Guard
MUGEROUN
THE CUTPURSE
LOREINE,—a preacher
SEROUNE
RAMUS
TALEUS
FRIAR
SURGEONENGLISH AGENT
APOTHECARY
Captain of the Guard, Protestants, Schoolmasters, Soldiers,
    Murderers, Attendants, &c.
CATHERINE,—the Queen Mother of France
MARGARET,—her daughter, wife to the KING OF NAVARRE
THE OLD QUEEN OF NAVARRE
DUCHESS OF GUISE
WIFE TO SEROUNE
Maid to the Duchess of Guise

THE MASSACRE AT PARIS.
With the Death of the Duke of Guise.

[Scene i]

Enter Charles the French King, [Catherine] the Queene Mother,
the King of Navarre, the Prince of Condye, the Lord high
Admirall, and [Margaret] the Queene of Navarre, with others.

CHARLES. *Prince of Navarre my honourable brother,*
Prince Condy, and my good Lord Admirall,
wishe this union and religious league,
Knit in these hands, thus joyn'd in nuptiall rites,
May not desolve, till death desolve our lives,
And that the native sparkes of princely love,
That kindled first this motion in our hearts,
May still be feweld in our progenye.

NAVAREE. *The many favours which your grace has showne,*
From time to time, but specially in this,
Shall binde me ever to your highnes will,
In what Queen Mother or your grace commands.

QUEENE MOTHER. *Thanks sonne Navarre, you see we love you well,*
That linke you in mariage with our daughter heer:
And as you know, our difference in Religion
Might be a meanes to crosse you in your love.

CHARLES. *Well Madam, let that rest:*
And now my Lords the mariage rites perfourm'd,
We think it good to goe and consumate
The rest, with hearing of an holy Masse:
Sister, I think your selfe will beare us company.

QUEENE MARGARET. *I will my good Lord.*

CHARLES. *The rest that will not goe (my Lords) may stay:*
Come Mother,
Let us goe to honor this solemnitie.

QUEENE MOTHER. *Which Ile desolve with bloud and crueltie.*

5

[Aside.]

Exit [Charles] the King, Queene Mother, and [Margaret]
the Queene of Navar [with others], and manet Navar,
the Prince of Condy, and the Lord high Admirall.

NAVARRE. Prince Condy and my good Lord Admiral,
Now Guise may storme but does us little hurt:
Having the King, Queene Mother on our side,
To stop the mallice of his envious heart,
That seekes to murder all the Protestants:
Have you not heard of late how he decreed,
If that the King had given consent thereto,
That all the protestants that are in Paris,
Should have been murdered the other night?

ADMIRALL. My Lord I mervaile that th'aspiring Guise
Dares once adventure without the Kings assent,
To meddle or attempt such dangerous things.

CONDY. My Lord you need not mervaile at the Guise,
For what he doth the Pope will ratifie:
In murder, mischeefe, or in tiranny.

NAVARRE. But he that sits and rules above the clowdes,
Doth heare and see the praiers of the just:
And will revenge the bloud of innocents,
That Guise hath slaine by treason of his heart,
And brought by murder to their timeles ends.

ADMIRALL. My Lord, but did you mark the Cardinall
The Guises brother, and the Duke Dumain:
How they did storme at these your nuptiall rites,
Because the house of Burbon now comes in,
And joynes your lineage to the crowne of France?

NAVARRE. And thats the cause that Guise so frowns at us,
And beates his braines to catch us in his trap,
Which he hath pitcht within his deadly toyle.

6

Come my Lords lets go to the Church and pray,
That God may still defend the right of France:
And make his Gospel flourish in this land.

    Exeunt.

[Scene ii]
    Enter the Duke of Guise.

GUISE. *If ever Hymen lowr'd at marriage rites,*
And had his alters decks with duskie lightes:
If ever sunne stainde heaven with bloudy clowdes,
And made it look with terrour on the worlde:
If ever day were turnde to ugly night,
And night made semblance of the hue of hell,
This day, this houre, this fatall night,
Shall fully shew the fury of them all.
Apothecarie.—

    Enter the Pothecarie.

POTHECARIE. *My Lord.*

GUISE. *Now shall I prove and guerdon to the ful,*
The love thou bear'st unto the house of Guise:
Where are those perfumed gloves which late I sent
To be poysoned, hast thou done them? speake,
Will every savour breed a pangue of death?

POTHECARIE. *See where they be my Lord, and he that smelles*
but to them, dyes.

GUISE. *Then thou remainest resolute.*

POTHECARIE. *I am my Lord, in what your grace commaundes till*
death.

GUISE. *Thankes my good freend, I wil requite thy love.*
Goe then, present them to the Queene Navarre:
For she is that huge blemish in our eye,
That makes these upstart heresies in Fraunce:
Be gone my freend, present them to her straite.
Souldyer.—

Exit Pothecaier.

Enter a Souldier.

SOULDIER. *My Lord.*

GUISE. *Now come thou forth and play thy tragick part,*
Stand in some window opening neere the street,
And when thou seest the Admirall ride by,
Discharge thy musket and perfourme his death:
And then Ile guerdon thee with store of crownes.

SOULDIER. *I will my Lord.*

Exit Souldier.

GUISE. *Now Guise, begin those deepe ingendred thoughts*
To burst abroad, those never dying flames,
Which cannot be extinguisht but by bloud.
Oft have I leveld, and at last have learnd,
That perill is the cheefest way to happines,
And resolution honors fairest aime.
What glory is there in a common good,
That hanges for every peasant to atchive?
That like I best that flyes beyond my reach.
Set me to scale the high Peramides,
And thereon set the Diadem of Fraunce,
Ile either rend it with my nayles to naught,
Or mount the top with my aspiring winges,
Although my downfall be the deepest hell.
For this, I wake, when others think I sleepe,
For this, I waite, that scorn attendance else:

8

For this, my quenchles thirst whereon I builde,
Hath often pleaded kindred to the King.
For this, this head, this heart, this hand and sworde,
Contrive, imagine and fully execute
Matters of importe, aimed at by many,
Yet understoode by none.
For this, hath heaven engendred me of earth,
For this, the earth sustaines my bodies weight,
And with this wait Ile counterpoise a Crowne,
Or with seditions weary all the worlde:
For this, from Spaine the stately Catholic
Sends Indian golde to coyne me French ecues:
For this have I a largesse from the Pope,
A pension and a dispensation too:
And by that priviledge to worke upon,
My policye hath framde religion.
Religion: O Diabole.
Fye, I am ashamde, how ever that I seeme,
To think a word of such a simple sound,
Of so great matter should be made the ground.
The gentle King whose pleasure uncontrolde,
Weakneth his body, and will waste his Realme,
If I repaire not what he ruinates:
Him as a childe I dayly winne with words,
So that for proofe, he barely beares the name:
I execute, and he sustaines the blame.
The Mother Queene workes wonders for my sake,
And in my love entombes the hope of Fraunce:
Rifling the bowels of her treasurie,
To supply my wants and necessitie.
Paris hath full five hundred Colledges,
As Monestaries, Priories, Abbyes and halles,
Wherein are thirtie thousand able men,
Besides a thousand sturdy student Catholicks,
And more: of my knowledge in one cloyster keep,
Five hundred fatte Franciscan Fryers and priestes.
All this and more, if more may be comprisde,
To bring the will of our desires to end.
Then Guise,
Since thou hast all the Cardes within thy hands

To shuffle or to cut, take this as surest thing:
That right or wrong, thou deal'st thy selfe a King.
I but, Navarre. Tis but a nook of France.
Sufficient yet for such a pettie King:
That with a rablement of his hereticks,
Blindes Europs eyes and troubleth our estate:
Him will we—

 Pointing to his Sworde.

But first lets follow those in France.
That hinder our possession to the crowne:
As Caesar to his souldiers, so say I:
Those that hate me, will I learn to loath.
Give me a look, that when I bend the browes,
Pale death may walke in furrowes of my face:
A hand, that with a graspe may gripe the world,
An eare, to heare what my detractors say,
A royall seate, a scepter and a crowne:
That those which doe behold them may become
As men that stand and gase against the Sunne.
The plot is laide, and things shall come to passe,
Where resolution strives for victory.

 Exit.

[Scene iii]
 Enter the King of Navar and Queen [Margaret], and his [olde]
 Mother Queen [of Navarre], the Prince of Condy, the Admirall,
 and the Pothecary with the gloves, and gives them to the olde
 Queene.

POTHECARIE. *Maddame, I beseech your grace to except this simple gift.*

OLD QUEENE. *Thanks my good freend, holde, take thou this*

reward.

POTHECARIE. *I humbly thank your Majestie.*

    Exit Pothecary.

OLD QUEENE. *Me thinkes the gloves have a very strong perfume,*
The sent whereof doth make my head to ake.

NAVARRE. *Doth not your grace know the man that gave them you?*

OLD QUEENE. *Not wel, but do remember such a man.*

ADMIRALL. *Your grace was ill advisde to take them then,*
Considering of these dangerous times.

OLD QUEENE. *Help sonne Navarre, I am poysoned.*

QUEENE MARGARET. *The heavens forbid your highnes such*
mishap.

NAVARRE. *The late suspition of the Duke of Guise,*
Might well have moved your highnes to beware
How you did meddle with such dangerous giftes.

QUEENE MARGARET. *Too late it is my Lord if that be true*
To blame her highnes, but I hope it be
Only some naturall passion makes her sicke.

OLD QUEENE. *O no, sweet Margaret, the fatall poyson*
Doth work within my heart, my brain pan breakes,
My heart doth faint, I dye.

    She dyes.

NAVARRE. *My Mother poysoned heere before my face:*
O gracious God, what times are these?
O graunt sweet God my daies may end with hers,
That I with her may dye and live againe.

QUEENE MARGARET. Let not this heavy chaunce my dearest Lord,
(For whose effects my soule is massacred)
Infect thy gracious brest with fresh supply,
To agravate our sodaine miserie.

ADMIRALL. Come my Lords let us beare her body hence,
And see it honoured with just solemnitie.

As they are going, [enter] the Souldier [above, who] dischargeth
his musket at the Lord Admirall [and exit].

CONDY. What are you hurt my Lord high Admiral?

ADMIRALL. I my good Lord, shot through the arme.

NAVARRE. We are betraide, come my Lords, and let us goe tell
the King of this.

ADMIRALL. These are the cursed Guisians that doe seeke our death.
Oh fatall was this mariage to us all.

They beare away the [olde] Queene [of Navarre] and goe out.

[Scene iv]

Enter [Charles] the King, [Catherine] the Queene Mother, Duke of Guise,
Duke Anjou, Duke Demayne [and Cossin, Captain of the Kings Guard].

QUEENE MOTHER. My noble sonne, and princely Duke of Guise,
Now have we got the fatall stragling deere,
Within the compasse of a deadly toyle,
And as we late decreed we may perfourme.

12

CHARLES. *Madam, it wilbe noted through the world,*
An action bloudy and tirannicall:
Cheefely since under safetie of our word,
They justly challenge their protection:
Besides my heart relentes that noble men,
Onely corrupted in religion,
Ladies of honor, Knightes and Gentlemen,
Should for their conscience taste such rutheles ends.

ANJOY. *Though gentle minces should pittie others paines,*
Yet will the wisest note their proper greefes:
And rather seeke to scourge their enemies,
Then be themselves base subjects to the whip.

GUISE. *Me thinkes my Lord, Anjoy hath well advisde*
Your highnes to consider of the thing,
And rather chuse to seek your countries good,
Then pittie or releeve these upstart hereticks.

QUEENE MOTHER. *I hope these reasons mayserve my princely,*
Sonne,
To have some care for feare of enemies.

CHARLES. *Well Madam, I referre it to your Majestie,*
And to my Nephew heere the Duke of Guise:
What you determine, I will ratifie.

QUEENE MOTHER. *Thankes to my princely sonne, then tell me*
Guise,
What order wil you set downe for the Massacre?

GUISE. *Thus Madame.*
They that shalbe actors in this Massacre,
Shall weare white crosses on their Burgonets,
And tye white linnen scarfes about their armes.
He that wantes these, and is suspect of heresie,
Shall dye, or be he King or Emperour.
Then Ile have a peale of ordinance shot from the tower,
At which they all shall issue out and set the streetes.

And then the watchword being given, a bell shall ring,
Which when they heare, they shall begin to kill:
And never cease untill that bell shall cease,
Then breath a while.

    Enter the Admirals man.

CHARLES. *How now fellow, what newes?*

MAN. *And it please your grace the Lord high Admirall,*
Riding the streetes was traiterously shot,
And most humbly intreates your Majestie
To visite him sick in his bed.

CHARLES. *Messenger, tell him I will see him straite.*

    Exit Messenger.

What shall we doe now with the Admirall?

QUEENE MOTHER. *Your Majesty had best goe visite him,*
And make a shew as if all were well.

CHARLES. *Content, I will goe visite the Admirall.*

GUISE. *And I will goe take order for his death.*

    Exit Guise.

    Enter the Admirall in his bed.

CHARLES. *How fares it with my Lord high Admiral,*
Hath he been hurt with villaines in the street?
I vow and sweare as I am King of France,
To finde and to repay the man with death:
With death delay'd and torments never usde,
That durst presume for hope of any gaine,
To hurt the noble man his sovereign loves.

ADMIRALL. *Ah my good Lord, these are the Guisians,*

That seeke to massacre our guiltles lives.

CHARLES. Assure your selfe my good Lord Admirall,
I deepely sorrow for your trecherous wrong:
And that I am not more secure my selfe,
Then I am carefull you should be preserved.
Cossin, take twenty of our strongest guarde,
And under your direction see they keep
All trecherous violence from our noble freend,
Repaying all attempts with present death,
Upon the cursed breakers of our peace.
And so be pacient good Lord Admirall,
And every hower I will visite you.

     Exeunt omnes.

[Scene v]
   Enter Guise, Anjoy, Dumaine, Gonzago, Retes, Montsorrell, and
   Souldiers to the massacre.

GUISE. Anjoy, Dumaine, Gonzago, Retes, sweare by
The argent crosses on your burgonets,
To kill all that you suspect of heresie.

DUMAINE. I sweare by this to be unmercifull.

ANJOY. I am disguisde and none nows who I am,
And therfore meane to murder all I meet.

GONZAGO. And so will I.

RETES. And I.

GUISE. Away then, break into the Admirals house.

GETES. I let the Admirall be first dispatcht.

GUISE. The Admirall,
Cheefe standard bearer to the Lutheranes,
Shall in the entrance of this Massacre,
Be murdered in his bed.
Gonzago conduct them hither, and then
Beset his house that not a man may live.

ANJOY. That charge is mine. Swizers keepe you the streetes,
And at ech corner shall the Kings garde stand.

GONZAGO. Come sirs follow me.

    Exit Gonzago and others with him.

ANJOY. Cossin, the Captaine of the Admirals guarde,
Plac'd by my brother, will betray his Lord:
Now Guise shall catholiques flourish once againe,
The head being of, the members cannot stand.

RETES. But look my Lord, ther's some in the Admirals house.

    Enter [above Gonzago and others] into the Admirals house,
    and he in his bed.

ANJOY. In lucky time, come let us keep this lane,
And slay his servants that shall issue out.

GONZAGO. Where is the Admirall?

ADMIRALL. O let me pray before I dye.

GONZAGO. Then pray unto our Ladye, kisse this crosse.

    Stab him.

ADMIRALL. O God forgive my sins.

GUISE. What, is he dead Gonzago?

GONZAGO. I my Lord.

GUISE. Then throw him down.

   [The body is thrown down. Exeunt Gonzago and rest above.]

ANJOY. Now cosin view him well,
It may be it is some other, and he escapte.

GUISE. Cosin tis he, I know him by his look.
See where my Souldier shot him through the arm.
He mist him neer, but we have strook him now.
Ah base Shatillian and degenerate,
Cheef standard bearer to the Lutheranes,
Thus in despite of thy Religion,
The Duke of Guise stampes on thy liveles bulke.

Away with him, cut of his head and handes,
And send them for a present to the Pope:
And when this just revenge is finished,
Unto mount Faucon will we dragge his coarse:
And he that living hated so the crosse,
Shall being dead, be hangd thereon in chaines.

GUISE. Anjoy, Gonzago, Retes, if that you three,
Will be as resolute as I and Dumaine:
There shall not a Hugonet breath in France.

ANJOY. I sweare by this crosse, wee'l not be partiall,
But slay as many as we can come neer.

GUISE. Mountsorrett, go and shoote the ordinance of,
That they which have already set the street
May know their watchword, and then tole the bell,
And so lets forward to the Massacre.

MOUNTSORRELL. I will my Lord.

   Exit Mountsorrell.

GUISE. *And now my Lords let us closely to our busines.*

ANJOY. *Anjoy will follow thee.*

DUMAINE. *And so will Dumaine.*

The ordinance being shot of, the bell tolles.

GUISE. *Come then, lets away.*

Exeunt.

The Guise enters againe, with all the rest, with their Swords drawne,
    chasing the Protestants.

GUISE. *Tue, tue, tue,*
Let none escape, murder the Hugonets.

ANJOY. *Kill them, kill them.*

Exeunt.

Enter Loreine running, the Guise and the rest pursuing him.

GUISE. *Loreine, Loreine, follow Loreine.. Sirra,*
Are you a preacher of these heresies?

LOREINE. *I am a preacher of the word of God,*
And thou a traitor to thy soule and him.

GUISE. *Dearely beloved brother, thus tis written.*

He stabs him.

ANJOY. *Stay my Lord, let me begin the psalme.*

GUISE. *Come dragge him away and throw him in a ditch.*

Exeunt [omnes].

[Scene vi]

 Enter Mountsorrell and knocks at Serouns doore.

SEROUNS WIFE. *Who is't that knocks there?*

 [Within.]

MOUNTSORRELL. *Mountsorrett from the Duke of Guise.*

SEROUNS WIFE. *Husband come down, heer's one would speak with*
you from the Duke of Guise.

 Enter Seroune.

SEROUNE. *To speek with me from such a man as he?*

MOUNTSORRELL. *I, I, for this Seroune, and thou shalt ha't.*

 Shewing his dagger.

SEROUNE. *O let me pray before I take my death.*

MOUNTSORRELL. *Despatch then quickly.*

SEROUNE. *O Christ my Saviour—*

MOUNTSORRELL. *Christ, villaine?*
Why, darst thou presume to call on Christ,
Without the intercession of some Saint?
Sanctus Jacobus hee was my Saint, pray to him.

SEROUNE. *O let me pray unto my God.*

MOUNTSORRELL. *Then take this with you.*

Stab him [and he falls within and dies].

Exit.

[Scene vii]

Enter Ramus in his studie.

RAMUS. *What fearfull cries come from the river Sene,*
That fright poore Ramus sitting at his book?
I feare the Guisians have past the bridge,
And meane once more to menace me.

Enter Taleus.

TALEUS. *Flye Ramus flye, if thou wilt save thy life.*

RAMUS. *Tell me Taleus, wherfore should I flye?*

TALEUS. *The Guisians are hard at thy doore,*
And meane to murder us:
Harke, harke they come, Ile leap out at the window.

[Runs out from studie.]

RAMUS. *Sweet Taleus stay.*

Enter Gonzago and Retes.

GONZAGO. *Who goes there?*

RETES. *Tis Taleus, Ramus bedfellow.*

GONZAGO. *What art thou?*

TALEUS. *I am as Ramus is, a Christian.*

20

RETES. O let him goe, he is a catholick.

Exit Taleus.

Enter Ramus [out of his studie].

GONZAGO. Come Ramus, more golde, or thou shalt have the stabbe.

RAMUS. Alas I am a scholler, how should I have golde?
All that I have is but my stipend from the King,
Which is no sooner receiv'd but it is spent.

   Enter the Guise and Anjoy [, Dumaine, Mountsorrell,
   with soldiers].

ANJOY. Whom have you there?

RETES. Tis Ramus, the Kings professor of Logick.

GUISE. Stab him.

RAMUS. O good my Lord,
Wherein hath Ramus been so offencious?

GUISE. Marry sir, in having a smack in all,
And yet didst never sound any thing to the depth.
Was it not thou that scoff'dst the Organon,
And said it was a heape of vanities?
He that will be a flat decotamest,
And seen in nothing but Epitomies:
Is in your judgment thought a learned man.
And he forsooth must goe and preach in Germany:
Excepting against Doctors actions,
And ipse dixi with this quidditie,
Argumentum testimonis est in arte partialis.
To contradict which, I say Ramus shall dye:
How answere you that? your nego argumentum
Cannot serve, Sirrah, kill him.

RAMUS. *O good my Lord, let me but speak a word.*

ANJOY. *Well, say on.*

RAMUS. *Not for my life doe I desire this pause,*
But in my latter houre to purge my selfe,
In that I know the things that I have wrote,
Which as I heare one Shekins takes it ill,
Because my places being but three, contain all his:
I knew the Organon to be confusde,
And I reduc'd it into better forme.
And this for Aristotle will I say,
That he that despiseth him, can nere
Be good in Logick or Philosophie.
And thats because the blockish Sorbonests
Attribute as much unto their workes,
As to the service of the eternall God.

GUISE. *Why suffer you that peasant to declaime?*
Stab him I say and send him to his freends in hell.

ANJOY. *Nere was there Colliars sonne so full of pride.*

    Kill him. [Close the studie.]

GUISE. *My Lord Anjoy, there are a hundred Protestants,*
Which we have chaste into the river Sene,
That swim about and so preserve their lives:
How may we doe? I feare me they will live.

DUMAINE. *Goe place some men upon the bridge,*
With bowes and cartes to shoot at them they see,
And sinke them in the river as they swim.

GUISE. *Tis well advisde Dumain, goe see it done.*

    Exit Dumaine.

And in the mean time my Lord, could we devise,

To get those pedantes from the King Navarre,
That are tutors to him and the prince of Condy—

ANJOY. *For that let me alone, Cousin stay heer,*
And when you see me in, then follow hard.

> *He knocketh, and enter the King of Navarre and Prince*
> *of Condy, with their scholmaisters.*

How now my Lords, how fare you?

NAVARRE. *My Lord, they say*
That all the protestants are massacred.

ANJOY. *I, so they are, but yet what remedy:*
I have done all I could to stay this broile.

NAVARRE. *But yet my Lord the report doth run,*
That you were one that made this Massacre.

ANJOY. *Who I? you are deceived, I rose but now*

> *Enter [to them] Guise.*

GUISE. *Murder the Hugonets, take those pedantes hence.*

NAVARRE. *Thou traitor Guise, lay of thy bloudy hands.*

CONDY. *Come let us goe tell the King.*

> *Exeunt [Condy and Navarre].*

GUISE. *Come sirs, Ile whip you to death with my punniards point.*

> *He kils them.*

ANJOY. *Away with them both.*

> *Exit Anjoy [and soldiers with bodies].*

GUISE. *And now sirs for this night let our fury stay.*
Yet will we not the Massacre shall end:
Gonzago posse you to Orleance, Retes to Deep,
Mountsorrell unto Roan, and spare not one
That you suspect of heresy. And now stay
That bel that to the devils mattins rings.
Now every man put of his burgonet,
And so convey him closely to his bed.

Exeunt.

[Scene viii]
Enter Anjoy, with two Lords of Poland.

ANJOY. *My Lords of Poland I must needs confesse,*
The offer of your Prince Elector's, farre
Beyond the reach of my desertes:
For Poland is as I have been enformde,
A martiall people, worthy such a King,
As hath sufficient counsaile in himselfe,
To lighten doubts and frustrate subtile foes.
And such a King whom practice long hath taught,
To please himselfe with mannage of the warres,
The greatest warres within our Christian bounds,
I meane our warres against the Muscovites:
And on the other side against the Turke,
Rich Princes both, and mighty Emperours:
Yet by my brother Charles our King of France,
And by his graces councell it is thought,
That if I undertake to weare the crowne
Of Poland, it may prejudice their hope
Of my inheritance to the crowne of France:
For if th'almighty take my brother hence,
By due discent the Regall seat is mine.
With Poland therfore must I covenant thus,
That if by death of Charles, the diadem

Of France be cast on me, then with your leaves
I may retire me to my native home.
If your commission serve to warrant this,
I thankfully shall undertake the charge
Of you and yours, and carefully maintaine
The wealth and safety of your kingdomes right.

LORD. All this and more your highnes shall commaund,
For Polands crowne and kingly diadem.

ANJOY. Then come my Lords, lets goe.

> Exeunt.

[Scene ix]

> Enter two with the Admirals body.

1. Now sirra, what shall we doe with the Admirall?

2. Why let us burne him for a heretick.

1. O no, his bodye will infect the fire, and the fire the aire, and so we shall be poysoned with him.

2. What shall we doe then?

1. Lets throw him into the river.

2. Oh twill corrupt the water, and the water the fish, and the fish our selves when we eate them.

1. Then throw him into the ditch.

2. No, no, to decide all doubts, be rulde by me, lets hang him upon this tree.

1. Agreede.

They hang him.

Enter the Duke of Guise, and Queene Mother, and the Cardinall [of Loraine].

GUISE. *Now Madame, how like you our lusty Admirall?*

QUEENE MOTHER. *Beleeve me Guise he becomes the place so well,*
That I could long ere this have wisht him there.
But come lets walke aside, th'airs not very sweet.

GUISE. *No by my faith Madam.*
Sirs, take him away and throw him in some ditch.

Carry away the dead body.

And now Madam as I understand,
There anre a hundred Hugonets and more,
Which in the woods doe horde their synagogue:
And dayly meet about this time of day,
thither will I to put them to the sword.

QUEENE MOTHER. *Doe so sweet Guise, let us delay no time,*
For if these straglers gather head againe,
And disperse themselves throughout the Realme of France,
It will be hard for us to worke their deaths.

GUISE. *Madam,*
I goe as whirl-winces rage before a storme.

Exit Guise.

QUEENE MOTHER. *My Lord of Loraine have you marks of late,*
How Charles our sonne begins for to lament
For the late nights worke which my Lord of Guise
Did make in Paris amongst the Hugonites?

CARDINALL. *Madam, I have heard him solemnly vow,*
With the rebellious King of Navarre,
For to revenge their deaths upon us all.

QUEENE MOTHER. *I, but my Lord, let me alone for that,*
For Katherine must have her will in France:
As I doe live, so surely shall he dye,
And Henry then shall weare the diadem.
And if he grudge or crosse his Mothers will,
Ile disinherite him and all the rest:
For Ile rule France, but they shall weare the crowne:
And if they storme, I then may pull them downe.
Come my Lord let's goe.

Exeunt.

[Scene x]
Enter five or six Protestants with bookes, and kneele together.

Enter also the Guise [and others].

GUISE. *Downe with the Hugonites, murder them.*

PROTESTANT. *O Mounser de Guise, heare me but speake.*

GUISE. *No villain, no that toung of thine,*
That hath blasphemde the holy Church of Rome,
Shall drive no plaintes into the Guises eares,
To make the justice of my heart relent:
Tue, tue, tue, let none escape:

Kill them.

So, dragge them away.

Exeunt.

[Scene xi]

Enter [Charles] the King of France, Navar and Epernoune
staying him: enter Queene Mother, and the Cardinall [of
Loraine, and Pleshe].

CHARLES. *O let me stay and rest me heer a while,*
A griping paine hath ceasde upon my heart:
A sodaine pang, the messenger of death.

QUEENE MOTHER. *O say not so, thou kill'st thy mothers heart.*

CHARLES. *I must say so, paine forceth me to complain.*

NAVARRE. *Comfort your selfe my Lord I have no doubt,*
But God will sure restore you to your health.

CHARLES. *O no, my loving brother of Navarre.*
I have deserv'd a scourge I must confesse,
Yet is there pacience of another sort,
Then to misdoe the welfare of their King:
God graunt my neerest freends may prove no worse.
O horde me up, my sight begins to faire,
My sinnewes shrinke, my brain turns upside downe,
My heart doth break, I faint and dye.

He dies.

QUEENE MOTHER. *What art thou dead, sweet sonne? speak to*
thy Mother.
O no, his soule is fled from out his breast,
And he nor heares, nor sees us what we doe:
My Lords, what resteth now for to be done?
But that we presently despatch Embassadours
To Poland, to call Henry back againe,
To weare his brothers crowne and dignity.

Epernoune, goe see it presently be done,
And bid him come without delay to us.

Epernoune Madam, I will.

 Exit Epernoune.

QUEENE MOTHER. And now my Lords after these funerals be
done,
 We will with all the speed we can, provide
 For Henries coronation from Polonia:
 Come let us take his body hence.

 All goe out, but Navarre and Pleshe.

NAVARRE. And now Navarre whilste that these broiles doe last,
My opportunity may serve me fit,
To steale from France, and hye me to my home.
For heers no saftie in the Realme for me,
And now that Henry is cal'd from Polland,
It is my due by just succession:
And therefore as speedily as I can perfourme,
Ile muster up an army secretdy,
For feare that Guise joyn'd with the King of Spaine,
Might seek to crosse me in mine enterprise.
But God that alwaies doth defend the right,
Will shew his mercy and preserve us still.

PLESHE. The vertues of our poor Religion,
Cannot but march with many graces more:
Whose army shall discomfort all your foes,
And at the length in Pampelonia crowne,
In spite of Spaine and all the popish power,
That hordes it from your highnesse wrongfully:
Your Majestie her rightfull Lord and Soveraigne.

Navarre Truth Pleshe, and God so prosper me in all,
As I entend to labour for the truth,
And true profession of his holy word:
Come Pleshe, lets away while time doth serve.

Exeunt.

[Scene xii]

*Sound Trumpets within, and then all crye vive le Roy two or
three times.*

Enter Henry crowned: Queene [Mother], Cardinall [of
Loraine],
Duke of Guise, Epernoone, [Mugeroun,] the kings Minions,
with
others, and the Cutpurse.

ALL. *Vive le Roy, vive le Roy.*

Sound Trumpets.

QUEENE MOTHER. *Welcome from Poland Henry once agayne,
Welcome to France thy fathers royall seate,
Heere hast thou a country voice of feares,
A warlike people to maintaine thy right,
A watchfull Senate for ordaining lawes,
A loving mother to preserve thy state,
And all things that a King may wish besides:
All this and more hath Henry with his crowne.*

CARDINALL. *And long may Henry enjoy all this and more.*

ALL. *Vive le Roy, vive le Roy.*

Sound trumpets.

KING. *Thanks to you al. The guider of all crownes,
Graunt that our deeds may wel deserve your loves:
And so they shall, if fortune speed my will,
And yeeld our thoughts to height of my desertes.*

What say our Minions, think they Henries heart
Will not both harbour love and Majestie?
Put of that feare, they are already joynde,
No person, place, or time, or circumstance,
Shall slacke my loves affection from his bent.
As now you are, so shall you still persist,
Remooveles from the favours of your King.

MUGEROUN. We know that noble minces change not their thoughts
For wearing of a crowne: in that your grace,
Hath worne the Poland diadem, before
You were withvested in the crowne of France.

KING. I tell thee Mugeroun we will be freends,
And fellowes to, what ever stormes arise.

MUGEROUN. Then may it please your Majestie to give me leave,
To punish those that doe prophane this holy feast.

He cuts of the Cutpurse eare, for cutting of the golde
buttons off his cloake.

KING. How meanst thou that?

CUTPURSE. O Lord, mine eare.

MUGEROUN. Come sir, give me my buttons and heers your eare.

GUISE. Sirra, take him away.

KING. Hands of good fellow, I will be his baile
For this offence: goe sirra, worke no more,
Till this our Coronation day be past:
And now,
Our rites of Coronation done,
What now remaines, but for a while to feast,
And spend some daies in barriers, tourny, tylte,
And like disportes, such as doe fit the Coutr?
Lets goe my Lords, our dinner staies for us.

Goe out all, but the Queene [Mother] and the Cardinall.

QUEENE MOTHER. *My Lord Cardinall of Loraine, tell me,*
How likes your grace my sonnes pleasantnes?
His mince you see runnes on his minions,
And all his heaven is to delight himselfe:
And whilste he sleepes securely thus in ease,
Thy brother Guise and we may now provide,
To plant our selves with such authoritie,
That not a man may live without our leaves.
Then shall the Catholick faith of Rome,
Flourish in France, and none deny the same.

Cardinall *Madam, as I in secresy was tolde,*
My brother Guise hath gathered a power of men,
Which are he saith, to kill the Puritans,
But tis the house of Burbon that he meanest
Now Madam must you insinuate with the King,
And tell him that tis for his Countries good,
And common profit of Religion.

QUEENE MOTHER. *Tush man, let me alone with him,*
To work the way to bring this thing to passe:
And if he doe deny what I doe say,
Ile dispatch him with his brother presently.
And then shall Mounser weare the diadem.
Tush, all shall dye unles I have my will:
For while she lives Katherine will be Queene.
Come my Lord, let us goe to seek the Guise,
And then determine of this enterprise.

Exeunt.

[Scene xiii]
Enter the Duchesse of Guise, and her Maide.

DUCHESSE. Goe fetch me pen and inke.

MAID. I will Madam.

    Exit Maid.

DUCHESSE. That I may write unto my dearest Lord.
Sweet Mugeroune, tis he that hath my heart,
And Guise usurpes it, cause I am his wife:
Faine would I finde some means to speak with him
But cannot, and therfore am enforst to write,
That he may come and meet me in some place,
Where we may one injoy the others sight.

    Enter the Maid with Inke and Paper.

So, set it down and leave me to my selfe.
O would to God this quill that heere doth write,

    She writes.

Had late been plucks from out faire Cupids wing:
That it might print these lines within his heart.

    Enter the Guise.

GUISE. What, all alone my love, and writing too:
I prethee say to whome thou writes?

DUCHESSE. To such a one, as when she reads my lines,
Will laugh I feare me at their good aray.

GUISE. I pray thee let me see.

DUCHESSE. O no my Lord, a woman only must
Partake the secrets of my heart.

GUISE. But Madam I must see.

He takes it.

Are these your secrets that no man must know?

DUCHESSE. *O pardon me my Lord.*

GUISE. *Thou trothles and unjust, what lines are these?*
Am I growne olde, or is thy lust growne yong,
Or hath my love been so obscurde in thee,
That others need to comment on my text?
Is all my love forgot which helde thee deare?
I, dearer then the apple of mine eye?
Is Guises glory but a clowdy mist,
In sight and judgement of thy lustfull eye?
Mor du, were not the fruit within thy wombe,
On whose encrease I set some longing hope:
This wrathfull hand should strike thee to the hart
Hence strumpet, hide thy head for shame,
And fly my presence if thou look'st to live.

Exit [Duchesse].

O wicked sexe, perjured and unjust,
Now doe I see that from the very first,
Her eyes and lookes sow'd seeds of perjury,
But villaine he to whom these lines should goe,
Shall buy her love even with his dearest bloud.

Exit.

[Scene xiv]
Enter the King of Navarre, Pleshe and Bartus, and their train,
with drums and trumpets.

NAVARRE. *Now Lords, since in a quarrell just and right,*
We undertake to mannage these our warres

Against the proud disturbers of the faith,
I meane the Guise, the Pope, and King of Spaine,
Who set themselves to tread us under foot,
And rend our true religion from this land:
But for you know our quarrell is no more,
But to defend their strange inventions,
Which they will put us to with sword and fire:
We must with resolute minces resolve to fight,
In honor of our God and countries good.
Spaine is the counsell chamber of the pope,
Spaine is the place where he makes peace and warre,
And Guise for Spaine hath now incenst the King,
To send his power to meet us in the field.

BARTUS. Then in this bloudy brunt they may beholde,
The sole endevour of your princely care,
To plant the true succession of the faith,
In spite of Spaine and all his heresies.

NAVARRE. The power of vengeance now implants it selfe,
Upon the hauty mountaines of my brest:
Plaies with her goary coulours of revenge,
Whom I respect as leaves of boasting greene,
That change their coulour when the winter comes,
When I shall vaunt as victor in revenge.

    Enter a Messenger.

How now sirra, what newes?

MESSENGER. My Lord, as by our scoutes we understande,
A mighty army comes from France with speed:
Which is already mustered in the land,
And meanesto meet your highnes in the field.

NAVARRE. In Gods name, let them come.
This is the Guise that hath incenst the King,
To leavy armes and make these civill broyles:
But canst thou tell me who is their generall?

MESSENGER. *Not yet my Lord, for thereon doe they stay:*
But as report doth goe, the Duke of Joyeux
Hath made great sute unto the King therfore.

NAVARRE. *It will not countervaile his paines I hope,*
I would the Guise in his steed might have come,
But he doth lurke within his drousie couch,
And makes his footstoole on securitie:
So he be safe he cares not what becomes,
Of King or Country, no not for them both.
But come my Lords, let us away with speed,
And place our selves in order for the fight.

    Exeunt.

[Scene xv]
    Enter [Henry] the King of France, Duke of Guise, Epernoune,
    and Duke Joyeux.

KING. *My sweet Joyeux, I make thee Generall,*
Of all my army now in readines,
To march against the rebellious King Navarre:
At thy request I am content thou go'st,
Although my love to thee can hardly suffer't,
Regarding still the danger of thy life.

JOYEUX. *Thanks to your Majestie, and so I take my leave.*
Farwell my Lord of Guise and Epernoune.

GUISE. *Health and harty farwell to my Lord Joyeux.*

    Exit Joyeux.

KING. *How kindely Cosin of Guise you and your wife*
Doe both salute our lovely Minions.

He makes hornes at the Guise.

Remember you the letter gentle sir,
Which your wife writ to my deare Minion,
And her chosen freend?

GUISE. *How now my Lord, faith this is more then need,*
Am I to be thus jested at and scornde?
Tis more then kingly or Emperious.
And sure if all the proudest kings beside
In Christendome, should beare me such derision,
They should know I scornde them and their mockes.
I love your Minions? dote on them your selfe,
I know none els but hordes them in disgrace:
And heer by all the Saints in heaven I sweare,
That villain for whom I beare this deep disgrace,
Even for your words that have incenst me so,
Shall buy that strumpets favour with his blood,
Whether he have dishonoured me or no.
Par la mor du, Il mora.

   Exit.

KING. *Beleeve me, Epernoune this jest bites sore.*

EPERNOUNE. *My Lord, twere good to make them frends,*
For his othes are seldome spent in vaine.

   Enter Mugeroun.

KING. *How now Mugeroun, metst thou not the Guise at the doore?*

MUGEROUN. *Not I my Lord, what if I had?*

KING. *Marry if thou hadst, thou mightst have had the stab,*
For he hath solemnely sworne thy death.

MUGEROUN. *I may be stabd, and live till he be dead,*
But wherfore beares he me such deadly hate?

KING. Because his wife beares thee such kindely love.

MUGEROUN. If that be all, the next time that I meet her,
Ile make her shake off love with her heeles.
But which way is he gone? Ile goe take a walk
On purpose from the Court to meet with him.

    Exit.

KING. I like not this, come Epernoune
Lets goe seek the Duke and make them freends.

    Exeunt.

[Scene xvi]
    Alarums within. The Duke Joyeux slaine.

    Enter the King of Navarre [, Bartus,] and his traine.

NAVARRE. The Duke is slaine and all his power dispearst,
And we are grac'd with wreathes of victory:
Thus God we see doth ever guide the right,
To make his glory great upon the earth.

BARTUS. The terrour of this happy victory,
I hope will make the King surcease his hate:
And either never mannage army more,
Or else employ them in some better cause.

NAVARRE. How many noble men have lost their lives,
In prosecution of these quell armes,
Is ruth and almost death to call to mince:
Put God we know will alwaies put them downe,
That lift themselves against the perfect truth,
Which Ile maintaine as long as life doth last:
And with the Queene of England joyne my force,

To beat the papall Monarck from our lands,
And keep those relicks from our countries coastes.
Come my Lords, now that the storme is overpass,
Let us away with triumph to our tents.

Exeunt.

[Scene xvii]
　　Enter a Souldier.

SOULDIER. *Sir, to you sir, that dare make the Duke a cuckolde,*
and use a counterfeite key to his privie Chamber doore: And
although you take out nothing but your owne, yet you put in
that which displeaseth him, and so forestall his market, and set up
your standing where you should not: and whereas tree is your
Landlord, you would take upon you to be his, and tyll the ground
that he himself should occupy, which is his own free land. If it be
not too free there's the question: and though I come not to take
possession (as I would I might) yet I meane to keepe you out,
which I will if this geare horde: what are ye come so soone?
have at ye sir.

　　Enter Mugeroun.

　　He shootes at him and killes him.

　　Enter the Guise [attended].

GUISE. *Holde thee tall Souldier, take thou this and flye.*

　　Exit Souldier.

Lye there the Kings delight, and Guises scorne.
Revenge it Henry as thou list'st or dar'st,
I did it only in despite of thee.

39

Take him away.

Enter the King and Epernoune.

KING. My Lord of Guise, we understand that you
Have gathered a power of men.
What your intent is yet we cannot learn,
But we presume it is not for our good.

GUISE. Why I am no traitor to the crowne of France.
What I have done tis for the Gospel's sake.

EPERNOUNE. Nay for the Popes sake, and shine owne benefite.
What Peere in France but thou (aspiring Guise)
Durst be in armes without the Kings consent?
I challenge thee for treason in the cause.

GUISE. Oh base Epernoune, were not his highnes heere,
Thou shouldst perceive the Duke of Guise is mov'd.

KING. Be patient Guise and threat not Epernoune,
Least thou perceive the King of France be mov'd.

GUISE. Why? I am a Prince of the Valoyses line,
Therfore an enemy to the Burbonites.
I am a juror in the holy league,
And therfore hated of the Protestants.
What should I doe but stand upon my guarde?
And being able, Ile keep an hoast in pay.

EPERNOUNE. Thou able to maintaine an hoast in pay,
That livest by forraine exhibition?
The Pope and King of Spaine are thy good frends,
Else all France knowes how poor a Duke thou art.

KING. I, those are they that feed him with their golde,
To countermaund our will and check our freends.

GUISE. My Lord, to speak more plainely, thus it is:
Being animated by Religious zeale,

I meane to muster all the power I can,
To overthrow those factious Puritans:
And know, the Pope will sell his triple crowne,
I, and the catholick Philip King of Spaine,
Ere I shall want, will cause his Indians,
To rip the golden bowels of America.
Navarre that cloakes them underneath his wings,
Shall feele the house of Lorayne is his foe:
Your highnes need not feare mine armies force,
Tis for your safetie and your enemies wrack.

KING. Guise, weare our crowne, and be thou King of France,
And as Dictator make or warre or peace,
Whilste I cry placet like a Senator.
I cannot brook thy hauty insolence,
Dismisse thy campe or else by our Edict,
Be thou proclaimde a traitor throughout France.

GUISE. The choyse is hard, I must dissemble.

   [Aside.]

My Lord, in token of my true humilitie,
And simple meaning to your Majestie,
I kisse your graces hand, and take my leave,
Intending to dislodge my campe with speed.

KING. Then farwell Guise, the King and thou art freends.

   Exit Guise.

EPERNOUNE. But trust him not my Lord,
For had your highnesse seene with what a pompe
He entred Paris, and how the Citizens
With gifts and shewes did entertaine him
And promised to be at his commaund:
Nay, they fear'd not to speak in the streetes,
That Guise ch, durst stand in armes against the King,
For not effecting of his holines will.

KING. *Did they of Paris entertaine him so?*
Then meanes he present treason to our state.
Well, let me alone, whose within there?

    Enter one with e pen and inke.

Make a discharge of all my counsell straite,
And Ile subscribe my name and seale it straight.
My head shall be my counsell, they are false:
And Epernoune I will be rulde by thee.

EPERNOUNE. *My Lord,*
I think for safety of your person,
It would be good the Guise were made away,
And so to quite your grace of all suspect.

KING. *First let us set our hand and seale to this,*
And then Ile tell thee what I meane to doe.

    He writes.

So, convey this to the counsell presently.

    Exit one.

And Epernoune though I seeme milde and calme,
Thinke not but I am tragicall within:
Ile secretly convey me unto Bloyse,
For now that Paris takes the Guises parse,
Heere is not staying for the King of France,
Unles he means to be betraide and dye:
But as I live, so sure the Guise shall dye.

    Exeunt.

[Scene xviii]

Enter the King of Navarre reading of a letter, and Bartus.

NAVARRE. My Lord, I am advertised from France,
That the Guise hath taken armes against the King,
And that Paris is revolted from his grace.

BARTUS. Then hath your grace fit oportunitie,
To shew your love unto the King of France:
Offering him aide against his enemies,
Which cannot but be thankfully receiv'd.

NAVARRE. Bartus, it shall be so, poast then to Fraunce,
And there salute his highnesse in our name,
Assure him all the aide we can provide,
Against the Guisians and their complices.
Bartus be gone, commend me to his grace,
And tell him ere it be long, Ile visite him.

BARTUS. I will my Lord.

Exit.

NAVARRE. Pleshe.

Enter Pleshe.

PLESHE. My Lord.

NAVARRE. Pleshe, goe muster up our men with speed,
And let them march away to France amaine:
For we must aide the King against the Guise.
Be gone I say, tis time that we were there.

PLESHE. I goe my Lord.

[Exit.]

NAVARRE. That wicked Guise I feare me much will be,
The wine of that famous Realme of France:
For his aspiring thoughts aime at the crowne,

He takes his vantage on Religion,
To plant the Pope and popelings in the Realme,
And binde it wholy to the Sea of Rome:
But if that God doe prosper mine attempts,
And send us safely to arrive in France:
Wee'l beat him back, and drive him to his death,
That basely seekes the wine of his Realme.

     Exit.

[Scene xix]

    Enter the Captaine of the guarde, and three murtherers.

CAPTAINE. *Come on sirs, what, are you resolutely bent,*
Hating the life and honour of the Guise?
What, will you not feare when you see him come?

1. *Feare him said you? tush, were he heere, we would kill him*
presently.

2. *O that his heart were leaping in my hand.*

31. *But when will he come that we may murther him?*

CAPTAINE. *Well then, I see you are resolute.*

1. *Let us alone, I warrant you.*

CAPTAINE. *Then sirs take your standings within this Chamber,*
For anon the Guise will come.

ALL. *You will give us our money?*

CAPTAINE. *I, I, feare not: stand close, be resolute:*

    [The murtherers go aside as if in the next room.]

44

Now fals the star whose influence governes France,
Whose light was deadly to the Protestants:
Now must he fall and perish in his height.

    Enter the King and Epernoune.

KING. *Now Captain of my guarde, are these murtherers ready?*

CAPTAINE. *They be my good Lord.*

KING. *But are they resolute and armde to kill,*
Hating the life and honour of the Guise?

CAPTAINE. *I warrant you my Lord.*

    [Exit.]

KING. *Then come proud Guise and heere disgordge thy brest,*
Surchargde with surfet of ambitious thoughts:
Breath out that life wherein my death was hid,
And end thy endles treasons with thy death.

    Enter the Guise [within] and knocketh.

GUISE. *Holla varlet, hey: Epernoune, where is the King?*

EPERNOUNE. *Mounted his royall Cabonet.*

GUISE. *I prethee tell him that the Guise is heere.*

EPERNOUNE. *And please your grace the Duke of Guise doth crave*
Accesse unto your highnes.

KING. *Let him come in.*
Come Guise and see thy traiterous guile outreacht,
And perish in the pit thou mad'st for me.

    The Guise comes to the King.

GUISE. *Good morrow to your Majestie.*

KING. *Good morrow to my loving Cousin of Guise.*
How fares it this morning with your excellence?

GUISE. *I heard your Majestie was scarcely pleasde,*
That in the Court I bear so great a traine.

KING. *They were to blame that said I was displeasde,*
And you good Cosin to imagine it.
Twere hard with me if I should doubt my kinne,
Or be suspicious of my deerest freends:
Cousin, assure you I am resolute,
Whatever any whisper in mine eares,
Not to suspect disloyaltye in thee,
And so sweet Cuz farwell.

    Exit King [and Epernoune].

GUISE. *So,*
Now sues the King for favour to the Guise,
And all his Minions stoup when I commaund:
Why this tis to have an army in the fielde.
Now by the holy sacrament I sweare,
As ancient Romanes over their Captive Lords,
So will I triumph over this wanton King,
And he shall follow my proud Chariots wheeles.
Now doe I but begin to look about,
And all my former time was spent in vaine:
Holde Sworde,
For in thee is the Guises hope.

    Enter one of the Murtherers.

Villaine, why cost thou look so gastly? speake.

3. *O pardon me my Lord of Guise.*

GUISE. *Pardon thee, why what hast thou done?*

46

3. O my Lord, I am one of them that is set to murder you.

GUISE. To murder me, villaine?

*3. I my Lord, the rest have taine their standings in the next
roome, therefore good my Lord goe not foorth.*

*GUISE. Yet Caesar shall goe forth.
Let mean consaits, and baser men feare death,
Tut they are pesants, I am Duke of Guise:
And princes with their lookes ingender feare.*

2 MURD. Stand close, he is comming, I know him by his voice.

GUISE. As pale as ashes, nay then tis time to look about.

ALL. Downe with him, downe with him.

　　They stabbe him.

GUISE. Oh I have my death wound, give me leave to speak.

2. Then pray to God, and aske forgivenes of the King.

*GUISE. Trouble me not, I neare offended him,
Nor will I aske forgivenes of the King.
Oh that I have not power to stay my life,
Nor immortalitie to be reveng'd:
To dye by Pesantes, what a greefe is this?
Ah Sextus, be reveng'd upon the King,
Philip and Parma, I am slaine for you:
Pope excommunicate, Philip depose,
The wicked branch of curst Valois's line.
Vive la messe, perish Hugonets,
Thus Caesar did goe foorth, and thus he dies.*

　　He dyes.

Enter Captaine of the Guarde.

CAPTAINE. *What, have you done?*
Then stay a while and Ile goe call the King,

[Enter King and Epernoune attended.]

But see where he comes.
My Lord, see where the Guise is slaine.

KING. *Oh this sweet sight is phisick to my soule,*
Goe fetch his sonne for to beholde his death:

[Exit attendant.]

Surchargde with guilt of thousand massacres,
Mounser of Loraine sinke away to hell,
In just remembrance of those bloudy broyles,
To which thou didst alure me being alive:
And heere in presence of you all I sweare,
I nere was King of France untill this houre:
This is the traitor that hath spent my golde,
In making forraine warres and cruel broiles.
Did he not draw a sorte of English priestes
From Doway to the Seminary at Remes,
To hatch forth treason gainst their naturall Queene?
Did he not cause the King of Spaines huge fleete,
To threaten England and to menace me?
Did he not injure Mounser thats deceast?
Hath he not made me in the Popes defence,
To spend the treasure that should strength my land,
In civill broiles between Navarre and me?
Tush, to be short, he meant to make me Munke,
Or else to murder me, and so be King.
Let Christian princes that shall heare of this,
(As all the world shall know our Guise is dead)
Rest satisfed with this that heer I sweare,
Nere was there King of France so yoakt as I.

EPERNOUNE. *My Lord heer is his sonne.*

Enter the Guises sonne.

KING. Boy, look where your father lyes.

YONG GUISE. My father slaine, who hath done this deed?

KING. Sirra twas I that slew him, and will slay
Thee too, and thou prove such a traitor.

YONG GUISE. Art thou King, and hast done this bloudy deed?
Ile be revengde.

He offereth to throwe his dagger.

KING. Away to prison with him, Ile clippe his winges
Or ere he passe my handes, away with him.

Exit Boy.

But what availeth that this traitors dead,
When Duke Dumaine his brother is alive,
And that young Cardinall that is growne so proud?
Goe to the Governour of Orleance,
And will him in my name to kill the Duke.

[Exit Captaine of the Guarde.]

Get you away and strangle the Cardinall.

[Exit murtherers.]

These two will make one entire Duke of Guise,
Especially with our olde mothers helpe.

EPERNOUNE. My Lord, see where she comes, as if she droupt
To heare these newest

Enter Queene Mother [attended].

KING. And let her croup, my heart is light enough.

Mother, how like you this device of mine?
I slew the Guise, because I would be King.

QUEENE MOTHER. King, why so thou wert before.
Pray God thou be a King now this is done.

KING. Nay he was King and countermanded me,
But now I will be King and rule my selfe,
And make the Guisians stoup that are alive.

QUEENE MOTHER. I cannot speak for greefe: when thou went home,
I would that I had murdered thee my sonne.
My sonne: thou art a changeling, not my sonne.
I curse thee and exclaime thee miscreant,
Traitor to God, and to the realme of France.

KING. Cry out, exclaime, houle till thy throat be hoarce,
The Guise is slaine, and I rejoyce therefore:
And now will I to armes, come Epernoune:
And let her greeve her heart out if she will.

    Exit the King and Epernoune.

QUEENE MOTHER. Away, leave me alone to meditate.
Sweet Guise, would he had died so thou wert heere:
To whom shall I bewray my secrets now,
Or who will helpe to builde Religion?
The Protestants will glory and insulte,
Wicked Navarre will get the crowne of France,
The Popedome cannot stand, all goes to wrack,
And all for thee my Guise: what may I doe?
But sorrow seaze upon my toyling soule,
For since the Guise is dead, I will not live.

    Exit [the attendants taking up body of the Guise].

[Scene xx]

Enter two [Murtherers] dragging in the Cardenall [of Loraine].

CARDINALL. *Murder me not, I am a Cardenall.*

1. *Wert thou the Pope thou mightst not scape from us.*

CARDINALL. *What, will you fyle your handes with Churchmens bloud?*

2. *Shed your bloud,*
O Lord no: for we entend to strangle you.

CARDINALL. *Then there is no remedye but I must dye?*

1. *No remedye, therefore prepare your selfe.*

CARDINALL. *Yet lives*
My brother Duke Dumaine, and many moe:
To revenge our deaths upon that cursed King,
Upon whose heart may all the furies gripe,
And with their pawes drench his black soule in hell.

1. *Yours my Lord Cardinall, you should have saide.*

Now they strangle him.

So, pluck amaine,
He is hard hearted, therfore pull with violence.
Come take him away.

Exeunt.

[Scene xxi]

Enter Duke Dumayn reading of a letter, with others.

DUMAINE. *My noble brother murthered by the King,*
Oh what may I doe, to revenge thy death?
The Kings alone, it cannot satisfie.
Sweet Duke of Guise our prop to leane upon,
Now thou art dead, heere is no stay for us:
I am thy brother, and ile revenge thy death,
And roote Valois's line from forth of France,
And beate proud Burbon to his native home,
That basely seekes to joyne with such a King,
Whose murderous thoughts will be his overthrow.
Hee wild the Governour of Orleance in his name,
That I with speed should have beene put to death.
But thats prevented, for to end his life,
And all those traitors to the Church of Rome,
That durst attempt to murder noble Guise.

   Enter the Frier.

FRIER. *My Lord, I come to bring you newes, that your brother*
the Cardinall of Loraine by the Kings consent is lately strangled
unto death.

DUMAINE. *My brother Cardenall slaine and I alive?*
O wordes of power to kill a thousand men.
Come let us away and leavy men,
Tis warre that must asswage the tyrantes pride.

FRIER. *My Lord, heare me but speak.*
I am a Frier of the order of the Jacobyns, that for my
conscience sake will kill the King.

DUMAINE. *But what doth move thee above the rest to doe the deed?*

FRIER. *O my Lord, I have beene a great sinner in my dayes, and*
the deed is meritorious.

DUMAINE. *But how wilt thou get opportunitye?*

FRIER. *Tush my Lord, let me alone for that.*

DUMAINE. Frier come with me,
We will goe talke more of this within.

Exeunt.

[Scene xxii]
Sound Drumme and Trumpets, and enter the King of France,
and Navarre, Epernoune, Bartus, Pleshe and Souldiers.

KING. Brother of Navarre, I sorrow much,
That ever I was prov'd your enemy,
And that the sweet and princely minde you beare,
Was ever troubled with injurious warres:
I vow as I am lawfull King of France,
To recompence your reconciled love,
With all the honors and affections,
That ever I vouchsafte my dearest freends.

NAVARRE. It is enough if that Navarre may be
Esteemed faithfull to the King of France:
Whose service he may still commaund to death.

KING. Thankes to my Kingly Brother of Navarre.
Then there wee'l lye before Lutetia's walles,
Girting this strumpet Cittie with our siege,
Till surfeiting with our afflicting armes,
She cast her hatefull stomack to the earth.

Enter a Messenger.

MESSENGER. And it please your Majestie heere is a Frier of the
order of the Jacobins, sent from the President of Paris, that
craves accesse unto your grace.

KING. Let him come in.

Enter Frier with a Letter.

EPERNOUNE. *I like not this Friers look.*
Twere not amisse my Lord, if he were searcht.

KING. *Sweete Epernoune, our Friers are holy men,*
And will not offer violence to their King,
For all the wealth and treasure of the world.
Frier, thou dost acknowledge me thy King?

FRIER. *I my good Lord, and will dye therein.*

KING. *Then come thou neer, and tell what newes thou bringst.*

FRIER. *My Lord,*
The President of Paris greetes your grace,
And sends his dutie by these speedye lines,
Humblye craving your gracious reply.

KING. *Ile read them Frier, and then Ile answere thee.*

FRIER. *Sancte Jacobus, now have mercye on me.*

He stabs the King with a knife as he readeth the letter, and
then the King getteth the knife and killes him.

EPERNOUNE. *O my Lord, let him live a while.*

KING. *No, let the villaine dye, and feele in hell,*
Just torments for his trechery.

NAVARRE. *What, is your highnes hurt?*

KING. *Yes Navarre, but not to death I hope.*

NAVARRE. *God shield your grace from such a sodaine death:*
Goe call a surgeon hether strait.

[Exit attendant.]

KING. *What irreligeous Pagans partes be these,*
Of such as horde them of the holy church?
Take hence that damned villaine from my sight.

   [Exeunt attendants with body]

EPERNOUNE. *Ah, had your highnes let him live,*
We might have punisht him for his deserts.

KING. *Sweet Epernoune all Rebels under heaven,*
Shall take example by his punishment,
How they beare armes against their soveraigne.
Goe call the English Agent hether strait,
Ile send my sister England newes of this,
And give her warning of her trecherous foes.

   [Enter Surgeon.]

NAVARRE. *Pleaseth your grace to let the Surgeon search your*
wound.

KING. *The wound I warrant you is deepe my Lord,*
Search Surgeon and resolve me what thou seest.

   The Surgeon searcheth.

   Enter the English Agent.

Agent for England, send thy mistres word,
What this detested Jacobin hath done.
Tell her for all this that I hope to live,
Which if I doe, the Papall Monarck goes
To wrack, an antechristian kingdome falles.
These bloudy hands shall teare his triple Crowne,
And fire accursed Rome about his eares.
Ile fire his erased buildings and incense
The papall towers to kisse the holy earth.
Navarre, give me thy hand, I heere do sweare,
To ruinate this wicked Church of Rome,

That hatcheth up such bloudy practices.
And heere protest eternall love to thee,
And to the Queene of England especially,
Whom God hath blest for hating Popery.

NAVARRE. These words revive my thoughts and comfort me,
To see your highnes in this vertuous minde.

KING. Tell me Surgeon, shall I live?

SURGEON. Alas my Lord, the wound is dangerous,
For you are stricken with a poysoned knife.

KING. A poysoned knife? what, shall the French king dye,
Wounded and poysoned, both at once?

EPERNOUNE. O that that damned villaine were alive againe,
That we might torture him with some new found death.

BARTUS. He died a death too good, the devill of hell
Torture his wicked soule.

KING. Oh curse him not since he is dead.
O the fatall poyson workes within my brest,
Tell me Surgeon and flatter not, may I live?

SURGEON. Alas my Lord, your highnes cannot live.

NAVARRE. Surgeon, why saist thou so? the King may live.

KING. Oh no Navarre, thou must be King of France.

NAVARRE. Long may you live, and still be King of France.

EPERNOUNE. Or else dye Epernoune.

KING. Sweet Epernoune thy King must dye. My Lords,
Fight in the quarrell of this valiant Prince,
For he is your lawfull King and my next heire:
Valoyses lyne ends in my tragedie.

Now let the house of Bourbon weare the crowne,
And may it never end in bloud as mine hath done.
Weep not sweet Navarre, but revenge my death.
Ah Epernoune, is this thy love to me?
Henry thy King wipes of these childish teares,
And bids thee whet thy sword on Sextus bones,
That it may keenly slice the Catholicks.
He loves me not the best that sheds most teares,
But he that makes most lavish of his bloud.
Fire Paris where these trecherous rebels lurke.
I dye Navarre, come beare me to my Sepulchre.
Salute the Queene of England in my name,
And tell her Henry dyes her faithfull freend.

He dyes.

NAVARRE. Come Lords, take up the body of the King,
That we may see it honourably interde:
And then I vow so to revenge his death,
That Rome and all those popish Prelates there,
Shall curse the time that ere Navarre was King,
And rulde in France by Henries fatall death.

They march out with the body of the King, lying on foure
mens shoulders with a dead march, drawing weapons on
the ground.

FINIS.

Freeriver is a community project working to create a place for people to visit and potentially live, long-term, in peace, free from the normal stresses of modern life.

We aim to provide a place where people can spend time discovering themselves and discovering nature. We aim to focus on creativity, health and wellbeing. We plan to provide events and classes for people in the local area and enhance the community.

Please visit our website for more details

www.freerivercommunity.com
freerivercommunity@hotmail.com

Made in the USA
Las Vegas, NV
24 August 2023

76540390R00036